Enid Blyton's
Teddy and the E

ILLUSTRATED BY S. DEAKIN AND E. TURNER

A TEMPLAR BOOK

Produced by The Templar Company plc, Pippbrook Mill, London Road, Dorking, Surrey RH4 1JE

Text copyright © *Teddy and the Elves* 1949 by Darrell Waters Limited
This edition illustration and design copyright © 1995 by The Templar Company plc
Enid Blyton's signature mark is a registered trademark of Darrell Waters Limited

This edition produced for Parragon Books, Unit 13-17, Avonbridge Trading Estate, Atlantic Road, Avonmouth, Bristol BS11 9QD

This book contains material first published as *The Golliwog and the Wireless* in The Fourth Holiday Book
by Sampson Low, Marsten & Co Ltd, 1949.

Printed and bound in Great Britain

ISBN 1-85813-960-0

||•PARRAGON•||

There was a new radio in the playroom. It had only just arrived, and the children were very excited about it. They had never had a radio before. "You just press this button here to turn it on," Emma explained to her little brother John. She pressed the round, red button on the front. There was a little "click" and, to the great astonishment of the toys who were listening, a band started to play. Teddy stared at the radio in surprise. The rag doll almost fell off the shelf, and the yellow cat was so frightened by the noise that she hid behind the blue dog.

The children were delighted with their radio. It had been given to them the day before by their Uncle John.

"May Emma and I keep it on, Mummy?" asked John.

"Yes – but not too loudly," said his Mother. "And make sure you keep it somewhere safe," she added. "I had a nice little radio that I kept on the shelf in the kitchen and it has completely disappeared. So has my best blue and white egg cup, *and* some of my silver spoons. You haven't seen them, have you children? I can't think where they can have gone."

But the children weren't listening to their mother. They were busy twiddling the knob on the front of the radio, instead, to see what different music they could find.

The toys thought the radio was wonderful. They listened to it all that day and all the next, and so did the children. They heard all sorts of different music and sometimes people even spoke out of the radio. The toys simply could not understand how they got in there. At other times, someone played the piano, and that seemed amazing too. How could a piano get inside such a small thing?

At night, when the children had gone to bed, the teddy bear looked longingly at the radio.

"It's magic," he said to the others. "It must be magic. How else can it have all those people inside it? I wish I could open it up and see exactly what is in there. How do you suppose you open it, Rag Doll?"

"Don't even *think* of such a thing!" cried the rag doll in horror. "You might break it."

"No I won't," said Teddy, and he began to undo a screw at the back. The rag doll had to get the big sailor doll to come and help stop him.

"We shall put you inside the brick box, if you don't solemnly promise to leave the radio alone from now on," said the rag doll. Teddy didn't want to be put into the brick box, so he had to promise.

But the next night Teddy wanted to press the red button that made the radio play. "I want to see the light come on, and hear the music play," he said. "*Please* let me press the button!"

"What! And wake up everyone in the house and have them rushing in here to see what's going on?" cried Rag Doll. "You must be mad."

"But they wouldn't hear it," said the teddy bear. "Oh, do let me try. I promise to keep it quiet."

"You really are a very, very naughty teddy," said the rag doll. "You are *not* to press that button at all."

For the next two nights the teddy bear was quite good. But on the next night, he waited until the toys were playing quietly in the other corner of the room, then he crept over to the radio and pressed the button. The light shone inside and loud music began to play!

The toys were horrified! Clockwork Clown and Sailor Doll rushed over at once and pressed the button again. The light went out and the music stopped.

"Teddy! How naughty of you!" cried
the sailor doll. "If you're not careful
you will wake up the whole family.
If they catch us, we will never
be able to come to life
at night again!"
But Teddy didn't care.
"They wouldn't have
heard it," said Teddy.
"It is you, with your
big shouting voice,
that will wake
everyone up!"

And he ran off into the corner, squeezed himself under the children's piano, and refused to come out.

After that, Teddy wouldn't speak to any of the others, not even the little clockwork mouse who loved to chatter to him. It was very sad. Soon nobody asked him to join in the games, and the teddy bear began to feel very lonely indeed.

Deep down, Teddy knew that he should apologise to the sailor doll, and to all the other toys. But he was a proud teddy bear and he could not bring himself to say sorry.

Then one night, when the moon shone brightly outside the playroom window, Teddy could stand it no longer. He tried to join in with a game that the toys were playing, but they just ignored him.

Teddy was very upset. He walked away.

"Very well!" he called, over his shoulder. "If you won't play with me I'm going to find somewhere else to live!"

Out of the playroom door he went. The toys stared after him in horror. No toy ever went out of the playroom at night. Whatever was Teddy thinking of?

The moon shone brightly, and the teddy bear could see quite plainly where he was going. He went down the stairs, jumping them one at a time. They seemed very steep! He reached the bottom and looked round. Emma had sometimes taken him downstairs. He knew there was a room called the kitchen that had a nice smell in it. Which way was it?

Teddy found the kitchen door and squeezed round it. He was just about to cross the room when a shadow fell across the moonlit floor.

Teddy looked up in surprise. Had the moon gone behind a cloud?

No, it hadn't. It was somebody on the window-sill, blocking out the moon – and that somebody was climbing in the kitchen window! The teddy bear stared in surprise. Who could it be, coming in through the kitchen window in the middle of the night?

"It must be a robber!" thought Teddy in dismay. "They come in the night sometimes, and steal things. Oh, whatever shall I do? The toys will be even more cross with me if I make a noise and wake everyone up. Oh dear, oh dear, oh dear!"

Meanwhile, do you know who it was climbing in through the window?

Why, it was three naughty little elves.
They sprang quietly to the floor,
and were busy trying to open
the larder door.

Usually, they only came
to the kitchen looking for
bits of food – a slice of
currant cake, perhaps,
or some biscuits. But
sometimes, when they
were feeling very
naughty, they took
other things too.

Only the week before they had taken some things from one of the kitchen shelves and hidden them in the garden, but tonight they had only come to look for things to eat. Teddy watched as they started to fill their little knapsacks with food – sticky buns, pieces of cheese, and even some of Emma's favourite sweets.

Then one of the elves jumped up onto a shelf and started to pick up all sorts of other things for his sack – paper clips, a little key, a coloured crayon. Then he held something up that sparkled in the moonlight.

"Hello!" he said. "Look what I've found!" Teddy was dismayed to see that the elf was holding a beautiful ring which he quickly put into his sack.

"It must belong to Emma's mother," thought Teddy to himself. "She will be so sad to lose it."

And right there and then he decided that something must be done. So while the elves were still busy filling their sacks, Teddy slipped out of the kitchen and hurried upstairs as fast as he could go.

When he reached the playroom, he rushed through the door, panting. The toys looked at him in amazement.

"What's the matter? You look quite pale!" said the panda.

"Quick! Quick! There are three elves downstairs taking things from the kitchen!" cried the teddy. "We must stop them. Let's wake the humans up! Come on, make a noise everyone!"

All at once the toys started shouting. The panda growled as loudly as he could. The jack-in-the-box jumped up and down and banged his box on the floor. The toy mouse squeaked. But it was no good. No one could hear them.

No one woke up. Not a sound could be heard.

And then Teddy did a most peculiar thing! He gave a little cry, and rushed over to the radio. Before the toys could stop him, he pressed the little red button – and then he turned one of the knobs right round as far as it would go! The light went on inside the radio and a tremendous noise came blaring forth!

It was a man's voice, telling the midnight news; but the teddy bear had put the radio on so loudly that it was as if the man was shouting at the top of his voice.

"This will wake them up!" said Teddy.

And so it did! It also frightened the elves in the kitchen so much that they dropped the contents of their knapsacks all over the floor and made a terrible noise trying to scramble out of the window.

But by the time
Emma's father had got to the
kitchen, they had quite gone.

"Must be those mice again!" sighed Emma's father, staring at the mess on the floor. Then something shiny caught his eye and he was surprised to find a ring lying amongst the crumbs...

Upstairs in the playroom, Emma and John were turning off the radio.

"This is what woke us up, Daddy," said John when his father appeared. "The playroom radio. But who could have put it on?"

Nobody knew. But Emma caught a gleam in Teddy's eye as he sat by the toy cupboard. Could *he* possibly have turned on the radio? Emma knew quite well she had put him back into the toy cupboard that evening – and there he was, sitting outside it! If she hadn't been old enough to know that toys can't walk and talk, she would have felt sure he had been up to something!

"The elves have gone! They won't come back after that fright!" cried the toys once everyone had gone back to bed. "Good old Teddy! *What* a noise the radio made, didn't it?"

Teddy was delighted to find himself such a hero. He beamed all over his face.

"Perhaps we can all be friends again now," he said hopefully.

"Oh, yes let's!" cried all the toys together. "It's so much nicer."

"And perhaps every so often you'll let me turn the radio on at night *ever* so quietly," added Teddy smiling.

"All right," said the sailor doll. "You deserve a reward, Teddy. You really were very clever."

Everyone agreed. And now when he feels like listening to a little music, the teddy bear turns the radio knob – very gently – and the music comes whispering out. Emma and John *will* be surprised if they hear it, won't they?